D1670831

Penguin  Readers

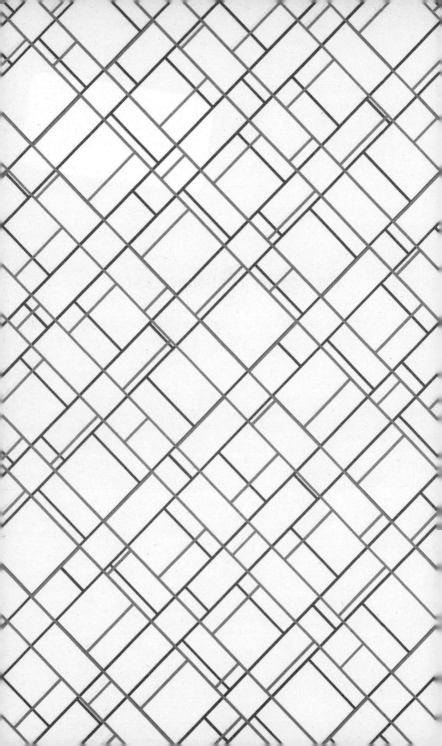

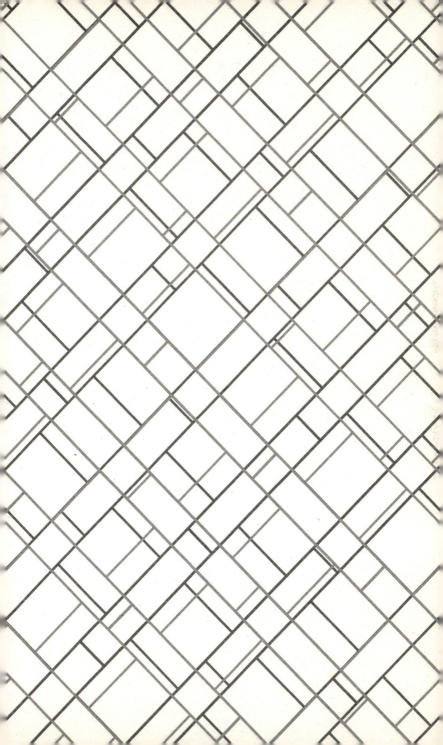

Penguin Readers

THE KISSING BOOTH

BETH REEKLES

LEVEL

4

RETOLD BY KATE WILLIAMS
ILLUSTRATED BY AMIT TAYAL
SERIES EDITOR: SORREL PITTS

PENGUIN BOOKS

UK | USA | Canada | Ireland | Australia
India | New Zealand | South Africa

Penguin Books is part of the Penguin Random House group of companies
whose addresses can be found at global.penguinrandomhouse.com.
www.penguin.co.uk   www.puffin.co.uk   www.ladybird.co.uk

Penguin
Random House
UK

The Kissing Booth first published by Corgi Books, 2013
This Penguin Readers edition published by Penguin Books Ltd, 2020

001

Original text written by Beth Reekles
Text for Penguin Readers edition adapted by Kate Williams
Text copyright © Beth Reeks, 2013
Illustrated by Amit Tayal
Illustrations © Penguin Books Ltd, 2020
Cover image copyright © Noordhoff

The moral right of the original author has been asserted

Printed and bound in Great Britain by Clays Ltd, Elcograf S.p.A.

A CIP catalogue record for this book is available from the British Library

ISBN: 978-90-01-73529-6

All correspondence to
Penguin Books
Penguin Random House Children's Books
One Embassy Gardens, New Union Square
5 Nine Elms Lane, London SW8 5DA

MIX
Paper from
responsible sources
FSC
www.fsc.org   FSC® C018179

Penguin Random House is committed to a
sustainable future for our business, our readers
and our planet. This book is made from Forest
Stewardship Council® certified paper.

Contents

CHAPTER ONE
My best friend, Lee

"Do you want a drink, Elle?" Lee called from the kitchen as I shut the front door of his house. It was Friday after school.

"No, thanks," I called back. "I'll see you up in your room."

Lee's house was huge and it had everything, even a swimming pool outside. I was there a lot – it was my second home – but the only place I felt really, really comfortable was Lee's room. Like any other sixteen-year-old boy's room, it was a mess. There were clothes all over the floor, empty drinks cans everywhere and a half-eaten sandwich on the desk.

Lee and I were best friends. We were born on the same day and we grew up together. Our moms were best friends at college. My mom died when I was very young and our two families became even closer after that.

Lee soon came in with two cans of soda.

"I know you'll want some of mine later, so I brought you one," he said, passing me a can.

"Thanks, Lee," I said with a grin. He knew me so well. "Now, what about our booth for the school carnival? Have you thought of anything yet?"

Lee looked at the can in his hand. "How about that thing where you throw a ball and hit the cans?"

"I was thinking of that!" I said. "But someone's already doing it."

We thought of lots of ideas for the carnival, but none of them was any good.

"It's too hot to think in here!" I said. The spring sun was coming through the window. I started to take my sweater off, but I couldn't get it over my head. At that moment, the door opened and I heard someone come in. I pulled my sweater off at last, leaving my hair a mess. Lee's older brother, Noah, was standing by the door, staring at me.

"*Bad luck, Elle!*" I thought to myself. "*Could you look any more stupid in front of the most good-looking guy in the world?*"

Noah had dark hair that fell into his deep blue eyes. He was tall and strong. His nose wasn't quite straight because he broke it in a fight once, but that just made him more handsome. Noah often got into fights, but he was clever and always studied hard. He was the top football player in the school, too.

"Hey, Rochelle," Noah said.

"Hi, *Noah*," I answered, with my sweetest smile. He knew that I hated people using my full name. And I knew he hated people using his first name – only his family called him Noah. At school everyone called him Flynn – his family name. He stared back at me, but I just kept smiling. He was Flynn, the most good-looking boy in school, and I was just his younger brother's friend.

"Lee," Noah said, "Mom and Dad are out tonight, so we're having a party at eight."

"Cool!" Lee picked up his phone to invite our friends to the party. Noah walked off slowly, and I watched him go.

"Hey! Take your eyes off my brother!" Lee said, grinning. "I thought you didn't have a crush on him any more."

"Shut up! That was when I was twelve!" I said, pushing Lee away and laughing. "Come on, we need an idea for our carnival booth. Let's look on the internet."

I sat down at the computer and looked for "school carnival booth ideas". We read the list of things that appeared, but either everything was boring or we couldn't do it.

"Wait!" Lee said, just as I noticed something on the list. I jumped up from the chair and turned around to Lee. We had the same smiles on our faces.

"A kissing booth!" we said together, grinning.

"This is going to be great!" Lee said.

"We just need to find people to work the booth," I said.

"Right," Lee said. "I'm not going to be a kisser and neither are you!"

"No way! I don't want my first kiss to be in front of everyone at the carnival!" I agreed.

"So, we need four guys and four girls to be the kissers," Lee said, and he picked up his phone again to start asking people.

Nobody was home when I got back from Lee's, but I wasn't surprised. My ten-year-old brother, Brad, was playing soccer and Dad was taking him out for a burger after the game. I went up to my room and chose a dress for Lee and Noah's party. Then I put on some loud music and stood in the shower. When I looked at the dress again after my shower, I started to feel worried. I sat down in front of the mirror to do my hair, and then I put on the dress. I looked in the mirror again. My hair was OK, falling down my back, but was the dress all right?

While I was trying to decide, Lee sent me a message on my phone. "Where are you?" he asked. I had no time to change now.

I walked round to Lee's house, feeling uncomfortable

in my high shoes. There were already people outside and the front door was open. I went to the kitchen to get a drink.

"Hey, Elle!" I turned and saw four girls waving at me. I went over to them.

"Olivia says you and Lee are doing a kissing booth for the carnival," Georgia said. "That's so cool."

"I'm coming to your booth, for sure," Candice said. "I heard Jon Fletcher's doing it."

"Do you know who you should ask to do it?" Olivia said. "Flynn!"

I laughed. "He won't."

"You have to ask him! If Flynn does it, every girl in the school will come to the carnival," Olivia said. "And you'll be so famous."

"Look, he's over there. Go and get us some drinks and ask him while you're there. Please try," Faith said.

"Fine," I said. I went over to Noah, who was standing near the fridge. I opened the fridge door to get some cans of beer.

"Will you do our kissing booth for us? Please? We can't find a fourth guy."

"You want me to be a kisser? At your kissing booth?"

I picked up two cans and put them under my arm. I had another three cans in my hands. "Please, Noah! It's for charity. And every girl in the school wants you to do it."

"That's why I'm going to say no. Sorry." He looked over at Olivia, Georgia, Candice and Faith. "You don't *need* me to do it, do you? They just want me to, right?"

I nodded. "Oh, forget it," I said, and turned away quickly.

"Wait a minute, Rochelle," Noah said and caught my arm. "What are you doing with those beers? You're too young to drink those."

As he held my arm, the cans under it began to fall. I tried to stop them, but my hands were already full with the other beers and I heard them fall noisily to the floor. At that moment, someone pushed past me to get to the fridge. Next thing I knew, I was dropping the other beers and falling toward Noah.

For a moment I found myself staring into his deep blue eyes. My heart jumped. "*Elle, stop that!*" I said to myself. But my heart did not calm down.

"Elle," Noah said, with a playful smile, "you know you're crushing me?"

"Oh, right, sorry!" I said, as he helped me back on my feet.

"Are you OK?" he asked.

"Fine," I said, hoping he didn't notice my bright red face. I turned away quickly.

Just then, Lee came over. "Oh, Elle!" he said, helping me to pick up the cans. "What am I going to do with you?"

"Get me out of here?" I replied hopefully, and he laughed. We left the beer in the kitchen and went through to the living room together to join in the dancing.

I tried to forget about what happened with Noah. Noah only saw me as the annoying girl who was his brother's best friend. I was nothing more than that to him, I was sure.

CHAPTER TWO
The worst Monday ever

It was Monday morning. I hated Mondays, but this one was the worst ever. My alarm always went off twenty minutes earlier than I needed it, because I hated getting out of bed. At last I got up and started to get ready. I was pulling on my school trousers when there was a horrible noise. The small hole in the right leg was now huge. And the only other thing I had to wear was my old school skirt, which was much too short. I looked ridiculous.

When I got downstairs, I had to explain to Dad why I was wearing my old skirt.

"I know I look stupid, but I have no choice – my trousers have a big hole in them," I told him.

My little brother, Brad, just laughed when he saw me. And Lee stared as I got into his car for a ride to school.

The boys at school stared too when I got out of the car.

"Hey, nice skirt," Dixon said, with a stupid grin.

I knew he was only having a laugh, but I was annoyed. As I walked past him toward a group of girls, I heard Adam, one of the football players, say something.

"What did you say?" I asked, angrily.

"Looking good! You should wear that every day," Adam said. Some of the boys laughed. Then Adam put his hand on my waist.

"Get off me!" I said.

"Leave her alone!" Lee yelled.

Then suddenly, Noah was there, Adam was on the ground and the boys were shouting, "Fight! Fight! Fight!" Of course it *had* to be Noah who hit Adam. Adam got back on his feet and then they really were fighting. Adam's lip was cut.

"Noah!" I yelled, but he wasn't listening. "Lee! Do something!"

Just then we heard the principal coming through the crowd. "Noah!" he shouted. "What's all this about? Noah, Adam, Rochelle – my office, now!"

Noah and I sat outside the principal's office, waiting our turn, while Adam was inside.

17

"I didn't like what Adam was doing," Noah said to me.

"Well, thank you, but I didn't need you to do anything," I replied. "Lee and I were fine."

"No one should talk to a girl like that . . . and if that girl is you . . ." He ran his fingers through his hair.

"*What's he going to say next?*" I thought, feeling my face turn red.

"I guess I want to look after you – you're like a little sister to me," Noah finished.

"Of course," I said, trying not to care.

We sat in silence for a while, but it was a nice, comfortable silence, which surprised me. I couldn't remember being alone with Noah like this before.

Adam came out of the principal's office. "Good luck," I said, when Noah went in, and he smiled back.

"You're talking to Flynn, remember – I don't need luck!"

When he came out, he gave me another smile but said nothing. The principal called me into the office. I was worried about getting into trouble, but the principal just wanted to hear my side of the story.

———

At lunchtime, the girls wanted to know everything.

"So, what's going on with you and Flynn?" Olivia asked.

"Nothing!" I said. "What do you mean?"

"You call him Noah, not Flynn," Olivia said.

"I've always called him Noah. I grew up with him around. He thinks of me as his little sister."

Luckily I had a message on my phone right then from Lee: *Come to the art room. I need some help!*

"Sorry, guys, I have to go. Lee's making the sign for our kissing booth and he needs me."

———————

In English class the next day, Cody waved at me to sit next to him. "I heard about the fight yesterday," he said.

"Oh," I laughed nervously, not sure what to say.

"Is it true you and Lee are doing a kissing booth for the carnival?" Cody asked. I nodded.

"Great. Are you going to be working it then?"

"No way," I laughed. "I'm not!"

"Too bad," Cody said. "You don't want to . . . you know . . . see a movie or something . . . with me?"

"Why not?" I said. "Wait, I don't have your number."

Cody picked up a pen, took my arm and turned it over. He wrote his number on my arm.

"Why didn't you just put it in my phone?" I asked.

"There's no fun in that," he said.

I told Lee my news in the car on the way home. "Hey, guess what happened in my English class. I was asked on my first date!"

"By Cody, right?" Lee said.

"School gossip!" I said. "Is there anything that anyone doesn't know?"

"Dixon texted me. Cody's a nice guy," Lee said. "But what's Noah going to say?"

19

"Why should your brother care?" I said.

"He just wants to look after you." We were outside Lee's house now. "You go in and start our music list for the booth," he told me. "Mom wants some things from the store. I won't be long."

I went into Lee's kitchen to get a drink. As I was reaching into the fridge for a can of soda, Noah came in.

"What's that on your arm?" he asked, sounding annoyed. I didn't answer. "Is it true you have a date with Cody?" he went on.

"I don't need to tell you," I said angrily.

"Do you even know the guy?" Noah said.

"No, not really. So I'm going on a date to get to know him. That's what people do, Noah." I was getting more and more annoyed.

"You're just too nice, Elle. You should be more careful."

"Noah, why do you care? You're not my dad or my big brother, you know!" I was feeling really angry now.

"I'm just trying to look after you!" he shouted back.

"I don't need looking after!" I yelled, and pushed past him out of the room to wait for Lee upstairs.

CHAPTER THREE
My first date

The week passed quickly, and Lee and I worked hard to get our booth ready. We made a music list and bought some pink and red decorations. Now we just had to finish making the sign at school. I did my best to keep away from Noah when I was at Lee's house. I was still angry and I didn't want to argue with him again.

Friday came and I was nervous about my date with Cody. I had no idea what to wear on a date to the movies. But I couldn't ask the girls and tell them that it was my first date. In the end I decided on a pink sweater and dark gray jeans. I checked the clock. I was already five minutes late. I ran downstairs and shouted goodbye to Dad.

"Have fun!" he called back from the living room.

Lee's car was already outside. I ran and climbed in.

"Sorry, but it's OK to keep Cody waiting a bit, isn't it?" I said, and then looked over at Lee. But it wasn't Lee. "Noah! What are you doing here?"

"Lee had something to do for Mom, which means I have to be your driver."

"You didn't have to – there are cabs, you know. So why didn't Lee text me?"

"I don't know." We sat in silence for a while. I felt nervous about the date.

"Do I look OK?" I asked Noah. "I've never done this before."

"You look nice. You'll be careful, won't you, Elle?"

"Of course. I can look after myself, you know."

"Right."

"I think I've spoken to you more in the past week than in all of the last year," I said. I looked over at him. There was nothing between us, I was sure. But he was really good-looking – with his hair falling into his eyes like that.

"*Wait a minute, Elle! You're going on a date with another guy!*" I said to myself. "*Stop dreaming!*"

"You can stop here. Thanks for the ride, Noah," I said.

"Fine. Do you need a ride home?" he asked.

"Cody will take me. If he can't, I'll call my dad."

When I got to the movie theater, I couldn't see Cody anywhere. I checked inside, but he wasn't there either. I waited outside, looking at my phone like I was doing something important. I hoped I didn't look as nervous as I felt.

"Isn't he coming?"

I jumped. It was Noah. Why was he still here?

"You really frightened me! Actually, he's just a bit late."

"And I thought you wanted to keep Cody waiting," Noah said.

"Noah, go home. It's fine." We stood for a while, not speaking.

"Hey!" someone said and I looked round. It was Cody at last.

Noah gave him the coldest look that I've ever seen and then got into his car and drove off.

"Sorry, the traffic's terrible," Cody explained. "What was Flynn doing here? I didn't know you two were close."

"We're not. Lee couldn't give me a ride, so Noah did."

"Right. Shall we go in?"

The movie started, but I couldn't stop thinking about Cody. "*Is he going to put his arm around me? Or hold my hand? Or try to kiss me?*" But he didn't do any of those things.

Maybe he was just as nervous as I was. After the movie, we went out to Cody's car and he gave me a ride home. We talked about movies and music, and discovered that we liked completely different things.

"Well, thanks, Cody," I said when we arrived at my house. "I had a nice time."

"Yeah. We should do this again sometime," he said. Then he looked at my mouth and moved toward me. "*He's going to kiss me,*" I thought. "*My first kiss. With Cody Kennedy. I'm not ready for this!*"

He moved closer. I turned my head quickly and kissed his cheek. And then I got out of the car as fast as I could, smiled, waved, and walked to my front door.

"*Elle, you're so stupid!*" I thought. "*It's lucky that you're not working the kissing booth!*"

———————

Of course, over the weekend, I told Lee everything about my date with Cody. Then in the car on Monday morning Lee said, "If you haven't heard from Cody by now, then he's not interested."

"Really?" I said. "But that's OK. I guess I only agreed to go on the date to be nice to him."

"You see, Elle? You're too nice!" Lee told me.

"Not to Noah!" I said. "Hey, why didn't you tell me he was giving me a ride?"

"I'm sorry, I forgot. Luckily you didn't kill him!"

"No, but Noah really looked like he wanted to kill Cody!"

As soon as we got out of the car at school, a group of girls came up to me.

"Everyone's talking about your date."

"Is it true that you didn't kiss Cody?"

"Why didn't you kiss him?"

Lee laughed. "See you later, Elle. And don't forget we're painting the sign for the booth after school."

Lee was getting out the paint and paintbrushes when I joined him in the art room after school.

"So, did you see Cody? How was it?" he asked me while we were painting.

I put my brush into the can of pink paint again. "We agreed we should just stay friends. It's fine, really."

Suddenly Lee dropped his paintbrush into the can of paint. The paint flew up over my shirt, my face, my hair.

"Lee!" I screamed. Lee started laughing. "It's not funny!" I yelled at him.

"Yes, it is. You should see yourself!" He couldn't stop laughing.

I hurried out to clean myself up. But as I was walking down the hall to the restrooms, a group of football players came toward me. They all started laughing.

"You look like a Picasso!" one of them said.

"What happened?" another added. "You should be on the wall!"

"Very funny," I said and turned away. Just then, a hand caught my arm and I looked round.

"What are you doing?" Noah said. "Why are you walking around like that?"

"Why should you care?" I said, but I was thinking about how good he looked in his football clothes. I pushed past him to the door of the girls' restrooms.

"Elle, wait! Lee just texted me – he wants me to give you a ride home. He's going for some food with Dixon."

"Sure." I tried not to think how ridiculous I looked, standing there with paint all over me. "I can get cleaned up at home."

I was nervous about being alone in the car with Noah. What if he asked about my date with Cody?

"How's the booth going?" he asked, as we walked out of school. I felt like I should be angry with him, but now I couldn't think why.

"It's going OK, but we still have a lot to do. And if Lee keeps painting me and not the sign, it will never be finished!"

"Well, you make a beautiful painting," Noah said. I looked at him. Did he mean that or was he laughing at me?

"Are you coming to the carnival?" I asked him.

"Sure. I have to really. But don't ask me again about working your kissing booth."

"OK, but will you come to the booth? It is for charity. And all the girls keep asking me to ask you – the thought of kissing Noah Flynn is just so exciting for them!"

"Well, tell them that I *might* come." We were in the parking lot, but I couldn't see his car anywhere. Then Noah stopped next to a red and black motorbike which I remembered seeing in their garage.

"I'm not getting on that," I said. I was terrified. "I've never been on a motorbike."

"You'll be fine, Elle. Here, have the helmet."

"You only have one helmet?" I said.

"It's OK. I haven't had an accident yet," he said. "Come on, get on. It won't bite."

What could I do? I had to get home to wash and change into clean clothes. Noah put the helmet over my head, his fingers touching my cheeks a little as he did it.

"Don't look so frightened," he said, and gave me a real smile. My heart jumped. He got onto the bike and I climbed on behind him. Then he reached back, pulled my arms around his waist, and started the bike. We began to move. I was terrified. I wanted to yell, "Slow down! You're going to kill us!" but I couldn't speak. We flew down the road, racing between the cars and trucks. My hair blew into my face from under the helmet, and I could hear nothing but the wind in my ears and the noise of the motorbike.

When Noah stopped the bike outside my house, I couldn't move. My arms were still holding onto his waist. Noah slowly pulled my arms away from him and I got off the bike. My legs were shaking as he undid the helmet and pulled it off my head.

"Your hair's all messy," he said, reaching up to touch it. "Now, don't tell me that you didn't enjoy that."

"I hated it," I told him. "I've never been so frightened in my life."

"What? You even hated holding onto me?"

"Shut up, Noah. And give me my bag. Please."

He passed me my bag and I walked up to my front door, my legs still shaking.

"Elle," he said. I turned around. "You have a little paint just there," and he pointed to his cheek.

I didn't answer. I went in and closed the front door loudly behind me.

CHAPTER FOUR
The kissing booth

By the end of Friday, the booth was finished, ready for the carnival on Saturday. Lee came to my house to get me at eight o'clock on Saturday morning.

"I hate mornings," I said. I was still half asleep.

"Here," Lee said, passing me a coffee. "Will this help?"

At school, we put the sign on our booth, and put up the pink and red decorations. We put some chairs inside, and checked the music. The booth looked really good. Then Rachel, a girl that Lee really liked, came over and started talking to him.

"I'm going to look around the other booths," I told Lee, so he could be alone with Rachel.

I really wanted this to go well for Lee. He didn't have a girlfriend and he never dated a girl for long. Usually his girlfriends didn't like Lee and I being together so much and broke up with him. I waited fifteen minutes, and then went back to our booth. Rachel and Lee were standing very close together when I walked up.

"Hi, Elle. Lee was just asking me to a movie," Rachel said. Her face was pink.

"That's great!" I said. Just then, the eight people who were working the kissing booth arrived. The four girls were wearing pretty dresses and the boys were in jeans and nice shirts. They all looked really cool.

"OK, so Ash and Dave, and Lily and Karen, you're first. The others will change places with you in thirty minutes," I told them. "It's two dollars a kiss, and Lee and I will take the money."

In front of the booth there was already a long line of girls on one side and boys on the other.

"All ready?" I asked. Lee started the music and grinned at me as we opened the booth. After twenty minutes both the lines were huge.

"Everyone's having a wonderful time. This is amazing!" I said to Lee, who was counting the money.

"And we've already made nearly two hundred dollars," he told me.

Just then, Karen came running out of the booth.

"I can't do it!" she said. "It's my ex-boyfriend. He's in the line!"

"But if you go, Lily will be on her own," I said.

Lee was looking at me. "You'll have to do it, Elle. Just until Karen's ex has gone."

"*I can't work the kissing booth! I've never kissed a guy in my life!*" I thought.

"No way! I can't!" I said.

"You have to – it won't be for long," Lee said, pushing me toward the booth. I walked up to Karen's empty chair in a dream. I looked at the line of guys in front of me. Lily smiled at me from the other chair and called, "Next!" A guy went up to kiss her.

Then I saw him. Not Karen's ex-boyfriend, but Noah,

waiting in line. He was next. He walked up to the booth and sat down opposite me.

"Since when were you working the kissing booth?" he asked.

"Since Karen saw her ex in the line. I guess . . . I guess he's gone. I . . . ." I was so nervous that I was having trouble getting my words out. I couldn't think. Was my first kiss really going to be with Noah Flynn? My best friend's big brother? The guy that could drive me crazy in three seconds. I stared at his mouth and I suddenly remembered falling into him in the kitchen at his party.

"I didn't pay two dollars to talk," he said, with a smile.

"*I don't have to kiss him if I don't want to. Nobody can make me,*" I thought.

He moved toward me, and then I was moving toward him. "*My first kiss . . .*"

He kissed me and I kissed him back. For a moment, I forgot about everything. I forgot that this was a kissing booth and forgot that people were watching us. I forgot that this was Noah, who annoyed me so much.

After the kiss, he moved back. I could hear people in the line talking about us.

"Wow," Noah whispered.

Someone touched my shoulder, making me jump.

"It's OK now, my ex has gone. You can go now," Karen said, looking annoyed. I nodded and stood up, still in a dream, and walked slowly out of the booth.

"Karen's back then?" Lee said to me, without looking up from his phone.

"I think . . . I think I just kissed your brother," I said, slowly.

"What? You and Noah? That's so weird! How did I not see that?"

"You were texting Rachel?"

Lee laughed. "You're right. But you two are not going to start dating, are you?"

"No, Lee! How could that work?"

"Yeah, if you date my brother and then break up with him, you might not want to be around me, either."

"Lee, I want to be your friend forever. I'll never do anything to hurt what we have."

"I know," Lee smiled. "Anyway, is it OK if I take Rachel to the movies tonight?"

"Sure, Lee. I'm happy for you. I'll ask my dad for a ride home." Then I remembered. "Oh no, Dad's taking Brad to soccer. But it's fine, you go and have a good time with Rachel. Really." The next minute, there was a crowd of girls around me.

"Is it true?" one asked.

"Did you and Flynn really kiss?" another one said. "Do you like him that way?"

Did I? I didn't know. Sometimes I hated Noah, but at the same time I liked him, too.

At the end of the carnival, Lee and Rachel went off together and I stayed to clean up. I counted our money – we had six hundred and fourteen dollars, which was more than any other booth.

"Lee's gone, so do you need a ride?" I looked around and saw Noah.

"*Oh no!*" I thought. "*Now I have to ride Noah's motorbike again!*"

"It's OK, I have my car. I know you hated the bike," he said, guessing my thoughts.

My heart started racing. "Sure," I said, trying to sound normal. I followed him to his car.

"OK if we stop at my house first?" he said. "My dad bought a video game for Brad, which I can give you."

"No problem," I said.

We didn't talk much in the car. Everything felt so weird and different. *"The kiss doesn't mean anything to him,"* I told myself. *"I know he's had lots of girlfriends. Kissing me was nothing special."* Then I knew that I wanted to kiss him again. *"That's not going to happen, Elle,"* I thought. *"Noah is Lee's big brother, who only sees you as a little sister. And remember, you're angry with him."* But it didn't really help. I still wanted to kiss him again.

We finally got to his house.

"I'll come in and get the game for Brad. Then I can walk home from here," I said. I didn't want to be in Noah's car any longer. I followed him into his kitchen and waited while he found the game. He came toward me with it. He was half a metre away from me. Then he was even closer.

Before I knew what I was doing, I reached up and touched my lips to his. Noah looked at me, surprised.

"Oh, I'm sorry . . . I mean . . ." I started, but he just kissed me again. I felt his hands on my back. Suddenly I realized what we were doing.

"Noah, we can't do this!" I said. "I don't want to be just another name on the long list of girls that you've kissed."

"Is that what you think of me?" Noah said. "You know, a lot of girls talk about kissing me when it isn't true."

He looked like he was telling the truth. And for the first time ever, he looked nervous.

"What do you want then, Noah?" I said. "We argue, and you're crazy – always getting into fights. And you're Lee's big brother. We can't be together. If Lee finds out, he'll be so hurt."

"Well . . . maybe Lee doesn't have to know," Noah said. "Elle, I can't stop thinking about you. You're the one girl that acts normally around me, and I like that."

"You said you saw me as your little sister. Why did you say that?"

"Because I thought you didn't want me back."

"I do want you." I couldn't believe what I was saying. All I knew was that I was reaching up to kiss him again.

"Promise me that Lee won't find out," I said. He nodded and kissed me back.

CHAPTER FIVE
My best friend's brother

I didn't stop smiling all the way home, but that night I lay in bed thinking. How long could it last? None of Noah's girlfriends lasted more than a week. No, I couldn't date Noah. We were too different and this was too wrong.

"*Remember, Elle,*" I thought. "*He's Lee's big brother! How can you ever tell Lee that you're dating his brother? When it goes wrong with Noah, what will happen with Lee? You can't hurt Lee – he's your other half!*"

But I didn't want not to be with Noah either, and when I thought about our kiss I felt warm inside.

On Monday morning, Lee gave me a ride to school, like he always did.

"Hey," I said with a grin as I climbed into the car beside him.

"Hi. What are you looking so happy about? It's Monday morning!" Lee said. "And I thought that you were worried about the kissing booth gossip."

"Well, I feel good, that's all," I said. I was thinking about kissing Noah and the texts that he sent me at the weekend. But I couldn't tell Lee that.

At school, I had a crowd of girls around me as soon as I got out of the car. They all wanted me to describe my kiss with Noah in the kissing booth.

"Did you actually kiss Flynn at the carnival?"

36

"What were you thinking about when you kissed?"

"Have you spoken to him since?"

"Do you still have a crush on him, Elle?"

"No way!" I tried to act normally and laugh at what the girls were saying. "I've known Noah all my life. He's just my best friend's big brother."

And that's what I tried to tell myself all week. Each time I saw Noah at school, across the hall or at lunchtime with his friends, I remembered the feeling of his lips on mine. But it wasn't right. He was my best friend's brother. I had to stop thinking about him. "*I must not kiss him again,*" I thought.

On Friday evening there was a house party at Warren's and Lee agreed to come and get me at 7.45 p.m. At 7.30p.m. I was still trying to decide what to wear when my phone rang. It was Lee.

"Listen, Elle. I'm really sorry, but Rachel asked me for a ride and . . ."

"Lee, it's fine – you go with Rachel. I'll ask my dad."

"No, I didn't mean that!" he replied. "All three of us can go together. I haven't forgotten about you!"

"Really, Lee, it's fine. You and Rachel should be alone together." I didn't want to get between Lee and Rachel.

"Are you sure? Wait a minute, I'll ask Noah to take you." Before I could stop him, Lee was calling out to Noah.

"It's fine. Noah will be there in twenty minutes," Lee told me.

"*Oh no,*" I thought. "*Just think of the gossip when Noah and I arrive at the party together!*"

I put on some jeans and a new black top, and looked at myself in the mirror. Did I look OK? I tried to tell myself that I wasn't thinking about Noah. As soon as I heard his car, I raced downstairs but Dad got to the door first. He looked very surprised to see Noah standing there.

"Just a minute, Noah," Dad said, and pulled me into the kitchen. "What's he doing here?" Dad whispered to me.

"Lee's taking his new girlfriend, so Noah is giving me a ride."

"Oh, OK. For a minute I thought you two were dating," Dad said.

I laughed. "What?"

"Well, be careful, Elle. I'm not sure about that boy . . . he gets into fights and he has that motorbike . . ."

"It's fine, Dad. He hasn't brought his bike tonight." I gave him a quick kiss on the cheek. "Bye!"

I walked with Noah to his car and we got in. He turned and looked at me. "You're beautiful, Elle, you know that?" he said. He moved toward me and then we were kissing. "*Elle! What are you doing?*" I asked myself. But in that moment I didn't care. I just wanted to kiss him.

"I've wanted to do that all week," he said. I hoped my cheeks didn't look as red as they felt.

"Everyone at school was talking about us at the kissing booth," I told him as we drove to Warren's. "It got really annoying. One boy wanted to give me two dollars for a kiss at school!"

Noah looked angry. "They shouldn't speak to you like that, Elle."

"It's OK, Noah. Calm down."

"You don't know what some guys are like. You're too nice. And some guys don't understand this and will think you like them. If you're not careful, you'll get hurt."

"Really, I can look after myself," I told him.

"*Here we go, we're arguing again,*" I thought.

When we got to Warren's, I went in first, so people didn't see Noah and me together. The living room was empty of sofas and chairs, and was now a dance floor with cool green and blue lights. I couldn't find Lee and Rachel at first, so after talking to some girls, I joined in the dancing.

Later in the evening, while I was dancing, someone behind me put their hand on my shoulder to dance with me. I turned around. It was a guy from school called Patrick.

"Shall we go outside?" he said, when the song ended. "There are so many people in here." He took my hand. Out in the garden, the night air felt cold after the warm room.

"Are you cold?" Patrick said, and he put his arms around me from behind. Then he tried to turn me around, and I thought he might kiss me. I started to push him away. Next thing, he was falling down onto the grass. I didn't know what was happening.

"Why did you do that, Flynn?" Patrick said, trying to get to his feet. "I only wanted to talk to Elle." In answer, Noah hit him again, really hard this time. Patrick was on the ground, holding his side and making a noise. Some people came out of the house to see what was happening.

"Come on," Noah said, taking my hand. "We're going."

"Noah!" I tried to say. "I don't want to leave the party yet. It's only 10.30!"

When we reached his car, I just stood by the door.

"I don't want to go anywhere with you," I told him. "I hate the way you get into fights."

He looked angry. "You have to leave before someone else tries to kiss you."

"I was OK, Noah. It wasn't that bad. And stop telling me what to do!" I said.

"I'm just trying to look after you!" he shouted.

"I don't need looking after!" I yelled back at him.

"Just get in the car, Elle!" he shouted, hitting the top of the car with his hand. There was silence.

"No, I'm staying here," I said, and walked away.

I didn't feel like going back to the party after that, so I called Dad. He just thought that I was tired and he didn't ask me any more questions.

On Monday morning at school, the crowd of girls was around me again.

"Why did you leave Warren's party early?"

"Did Flynn take you home?"

"I think Flynn has broken Patrick's rib!"

"His mom took him to hospital, you know."

"What?" I said and then I went straight to find Noah in the parking lot.

"Noah!" I yelled. The girls were staring at me, but I didn't care. "I can't believe it! You broke Patrick's rib!"

"He was annoying you. I told you before, I was trying to help. I saw you trying to push him off," Noah said.

"I didn't need your help. You hurt him over something stupid," I shouted angrily.

I felt someone touch my shoulder. "Calm down, Elle." It was Lee.

"Your brother broke someone's rib!" I said. "How can you think that's OK?"

"It's not OK that Noah gets into fights, but Patrick's rib isn't broken. His mom was worried and wanted the hospital to check it, but he's fine."

I looked at Noah. "I hate you sometimes, you know."

"I know," he said. And then something in his eyes made my heart jump.

"Elle, you're angry with him, remember," I thought.

I walked off quickly and Lee followed me.

"You looked like you wanted to kill him," Lee said.

"I can't do anything without him looking over my shoulder!" I said. "And don't tell me again that I'm too nice! I'm getting tired of people looking after me."

"Look, I know you're angry with Noah, but please don't get angry with me, too. Now, have you done the English homework? Because I need your help."

I smiled. Lee always knew how to make me feel better. I loved my best friend, I really did.

I stayed in the library at lunchtime. I didn't want to answer any more of the girls' questions about Noah. It was true that I really hated him getting into fights. But I realized I was also angry with myself because I was keeping a secret from Lee, my best friend.

At last it was time to go home. I waited for Lee.

"Hey, Elle."

When I turned around, Noah was there. "Elle, I'm sorry," he said. "I can explain."

"*Where is Lee?*" I thought. "*Why is he taking so long?*" Then I saw Lee and Rachel together, standing by her car. I texted Lee. "Are you coming?"

"Sorry, is it OK if I go to Rachel's?" he texted back.

"No problem," I replied, but I was a little annoyed.

Noah was watching me. "Do you need a ride home?" he asked.

"No, thanks," I replied.

"Elle, please don't be angry with me."

"But you almost broke Patrick's rib!"

"I know. I'm sorry I got angry and got in a fight with Patrick. Can you forgive me? Please, Elle. I'll take you home and we can talk. I have my car, not the bike."

I looked at him and I couldn't feel angry with him any longer. I nodded.

In the car, he said, "It's just . . . I care about you too much, Elle. And I *don't* think of you like a little sister."

He gave me a smile that made my heart jump. And then he was moving toward me and kissing me, and I was kissing him back.

CHAPTER SIX
Secrets and lies

The next two weeks went by quickly. Noah and I were together a lot, but we kept it secret from everyone. We went to the movies or met at his house when there was no one there. Lee was with Rachel a lot, too. When I did see Lee, all he wanted to talk about was how funny, how pretty, how nice and how clever Rachel was. So I was pleased that he never asked what I was doing.

I was really happy for Lee, and I loved being with Noah. What I hated was lying to my best friend, my dad, and everyone. But how could I tell Lee that I was dating his brother? I didn't have anyone to talk to about how I felt. I couldn't talk to Dad about things like this and, of course, I didn't have a mom to share things with.

———————

One Sunday evening, I was sitting in Noah's garage, watching him work on his motorbike. We were talking about the last movie we went to.

"Hey, Elle, can you pass me the wrench?" he said. "It's up there, above your head."

I climbed onto the chair and looked for the wrench. "Is this it?" I said, picking it up. But as I turned, the chair moved and I fell onto the floor. My face hurt really badly.

"Elle!" I heard Noah shout. He was next to me, pushing my hair out of my eyes. "Elle, are you all right?"

"It hurts," I said, touching my cheek. My fingers were red. "Is it bad?"

"It's not too deep, but we need to clean it," he said. He sounded worried. "Let's go into the house."

Noah helped me to stand up, and after checking that the others were still out, we went into the house. I sat at the kitchen table while he cleaned my face very carefully.

"Sorry," he said, when he saw that it was hurting.

"It's OK. You're doing a great job," I told him.

"I'm sorry you got hurt. Why did I ask you to pass me the wrench? It was a stupid thing to do." He was angry with himself.

"It's fine, really. It was an accident. And when did you learn to be a doctor?" I asked.

"Since I kept getting into fights. I had to learn to look after myself then."

"Oh," I said. "Why *do* you get into fights, Noah?"

"I don't know. When I was about fourteen, I started to get into fights at school. My parents were worried and they sent me to talk to someone about it. But it didn't help. I'm just a bad boy, I guess."

I liked it when Noah talked to me about himself. I felt closer to him because he was sharing something private with me.

"*But that's bad, Elle!*" I thought. "*You mustn't get closer to him because when it goes wrong it will be terrible. Lee will hate you and you will lose him as well as Noah.*"

But looking into Noah's eyes, all I could think about was him, and how much I liked being with him. How wonderful it felt when he had his arms around me. How bright and blue his eyes were. He moved closer to kiss me.

Suddenly, the door flew open and I heard Lee's voice. "What's going on?"

Noah jumped to his feet. Lee was by the door, looking from Noah to me. Then he noticed my face. "Elle, what happened?" he said.

Lee came closer to look at my face, then stared at his brother. "Did you do that to her?" he yelled.

Noah looked angry. "Of course not! I couldn't hit Elle."

"You might," Lee said. "Then how did it happen?"

"It's nothing, really," I said to Lee. "I'm OK."

"So what happened?" Lee yelled at Noah again.

"She was looking for you and she fell over something in the garage. Calm down, Lee. She's fine. It was an accident," Noah said.

"How can I believe you?" Lee shouted.

Noah looked angry now, and moved toward his brother. Lee looked ready to hit Noah, too. I jumped up and stood between them. They couldn't fight with me in the middle.

"Noah," I said quietly. "Noah, look at me. Please don't fight with Lee."

Noah turned toward me and I put my hand on his chest. "I'll never hurt you, Elle," he said.

Then I took Lee's hand and pulled him out of the room.

"Wow, I've never seen anyone calm Noah down like that before," Lee said. "You two are usually the ones who are arguing. So . . . what happened to your face?"

I hated lying to Lee, but I couldn't tell him the truth

when he was so angry with Noah. It wasn't the right time. I tried to remember Noah's story and tell Lee that.

"It really was an accident. I just fell over," I said.

"It's really weird, though. Since when were you two so friendly?" Lee said and looked straight at me.

My heart started to go faster. *Did Lee see Noah and I nearly kissing? I don't think he did, because I know Lee – if he wants to know about something, he usually asks. But I should tell him now before he finds out another way.*

But I didn't want to tell Lee about Noah. "He will hate me," I thought. So I said nothing.

"This isn't when you tell me my best friend and my big brother are in love, is it?" Lee asked.

"What? Lee, you're crazy!" I said.

"As long as Lee doesn't know, he can't be hurt by it," I told myself. *"So I just have to be sure he doesn't find out."*

———

For a while, everything went on as before. Noah and I were together as much as possible, and Lee knew nothing about it. At school Lee and I were busy planning the summer dance. It was going to be at the beginning of June, at the Royale, which was a really expensive hotel.

Inside, it was beautiful – everything was white and silver. We needed to plan the food, the music and the decorations. First, we decided that it was a masquerade – with everyone wearing masks. Lee helped me choose a new dress. It was a beautiful dark apple green,

with a full skirt, which just touched my knees. I loved it. We picked masks together, too, to go with our clothes. Mine was the same color as my dress with silver around the sides.

I was really excited about the summer dance, but I had no one to go with. Lee and I usually went to school dances together, but now Rachel was his date. I wanted to go with Noah, but of course I couldn't.

One day I was at Noah's, in the garage again, and Noah was working on his car.

"Who are you going with to the summer dance?" he asked me.

"I'm not sure – I don't have a date yet. Oh, did you know that everyone's going to wear a mask? We've decided that it's going to be a masquerade."

He nodded and went back under the car. "You should go with someone as a friend, not a date. Maybe Dixon?"

"Noah, you can't tell me who to go with! And why do you care?" I said.

"Of course I care, Elle. I want you to be *my* date."

I smiled to myself. "*Oh, I really want to go with him!*" I thought.

"Are you asking me to the dance? How's that going to work?" I said.

"Well, everyone's going to wear a mask, aren't they?" Noah said from under the car.

"*That might work, Elle . . .*" I thought. "*Or maybe you should tell Lee the truth!*"

Lee was worried about my date for the summer dance, too. "I'm sorry it's different this year, Elle," he said. "Hey, I've had a crazy idea. You could go with Noah! He won't have a date either."

"Don't be ridiculous!" I said, and tried to laugh.

"Wait a minute," I thought. *"Why not, if it's Lee's idea? Or you could tell him the truth, Elle!"*

"What's the matter, Elle?" Lee asked. "Are you OK?"

"It's Noah," I said.

"I knew it!" Lee said. "Is he worried about who's taking you to the dance? He's just looking after you, you know. And remember, he's leaving school soon and going to college. So he won't be around much longer."

I couldn't speak. Lee just thought Noah was looking after me, like before. And I didn't want to think about Noah going to college. It made me really sad.

"Do you know where he's going to college?" I asked.

"Maybe San Diego, but he's trying for Harvard, too."

I felt weird. I wanted Noah to stay close to home. I wanted to keep seeing him.

"But it will be easier if he goes away," I told myself. *"You can stop lying to everyone then, Elle."*

CHAPTER SEVEN
Lee finds out

A week before the school dance I still didn't have a date. Then one morning I saw Adam as I was walking to my next class.

"I heard you need a date for Saturday," he said. "How about going with me?"

"No, thanks, Adam."

"Come on, Elle. You don't have a date and neither do I." He moved closer to me.

"I don't want to go with you, OK?" I said. I didn't like the way that Adam was talking to me. He came a bit closer. Then we heard someone coming and Adam looked round.

"Get away from her," Noah said in a quiet but angry voice.

"Fine," Adam said. He looked a bit frightened. Noah and I watched him walk away.

"Are you OK?" Noah asked me.

"Sure. Thanks," I said. I knew that I should walk away, but I couldn't. I put my arms around him and reached up to kiss him.

Suddenly, someone was behind us.

"Elle! Noah! What . . .?" Lee started.

I jumped away from Noah. My heart was racing and my legs felt like they couldn't hold me up. Lee had his mouth open, unable to speak. I couldn't speak, either.

"*Oh no! Oh no! Why did he have to find out like this?*" I thought. "*Why didn't you tell him before, Elle? He's going to hate you forever.*"

"Noah?" Lee whispered at last, but he was looking at me. "Tell me this isn't what it looks like."

"Lee . . . you have to believe me. I didn't . . ." I tried to say.

"Elle, tell me the truth. Please."

"I'm so sorry, Lee . . ." I tried to take his hand, but he pulled it away.

"Elle, we've been best friends all our lives. We don't keep secrets. But you have lied to me!"

"Come on, Lee. It was difficult for her," Noah said, staying calm. "Leave her alone."

"You," Lee said. His voice was so angry it sounded strange. "I don't want to hear anything you have to say. You made her afraid of telling me."

Noah took a step toward Lee and pushed him into the wall. "It was her choice," he said.

"*Yes, it was your choice, Elle,*" I thought.

I looked from Noah to Lee. He looked back at me for a moment and his eyes were so sad. Then suddenly his arm flew out at Noah, pushing him away, and he walked off quickly.

I stared at Noah, and then ran after Lee as fast as I could.

"Lee, please wait!" I called. But he didn't stop.

Lee was the most important person in my life. He knew everything about me – all the things I loved and hated. He was my other half. I was terrified of losing him.

Lee reached the parking lot and stopped at last.

"Please, Lee," I said. "It's not like you think."

"Then what is it like?" Lee said. "You're my best friend and you have lied to me. My brother is more important to you than me. Do you have any idea how that feels?" Then he got into his car and drove away.

"*Oh, why didn't I tell him sooner?*" I thought. "*Why was I stupid enough to kiss Noah in school? Why did Noah and I ever get together? And is Lee ever coming back?*"

Noah was behind me and laid a hand on my shoulder. "Elle," he said.

"Just leave me alone," I said to Noah. I went back into school, and he didn't try to follow me. I didn't listen to any of the lessons for the rest of the day and Lee didn't come to any classes.

At home, Dad was busy, so he didn't notice that anything was wrong. But I didn't want to tell him anyway. I called Lee lots of times, but he wasn't answering his phone. I didn't answer any of Noah's texts. I didn't want to talk to Noah, only Lee.

Later, I tried to stop thinking about Lee, but it was hard. At eight o'clock I was doing my homework when the phone rang. Dad answered it in the other room. I knew it was Lee's mom, and that Dad was trying to calm her down. After a few minutes, he came into the living room.

"Noah's gone," he said. "He and Lee were arguing, and then Noah left. His mom doesn't know where he's gone, and he's not answering his phone."

"Did she say what they were arguing about?" I asked, feeling sick.

"Yes," Dad said. "It was about you. So can you please explain to me what's going on?"

"Noah and I . . . we . . . we were dating . . . in secret. Because I couldn't tell Lee."

My dad looked like he couldn't believe it. "But Noah? Of all the boys out there? Why him?"

"It all started at the kissing booth at the school carnival," I told him. I knew my Dad didn't like Noah much, so it was hard to tell him the truth.

"Are you in love with him?" Dad was saying.

"What? No! Of course not!" I said. "He makes me happy, that's all."

"Really? Are you sure?" Dad asked. I didn't say anything.

"Have you any idea where he can be? His parents are really worried," Dad said.

I shook my head.

I kept calling Lee, but he still wasn't answering his phone. Later, I couldn't sleep. I was worried about Noah, of course, but most of all I was worried about Lee. At midnight I turned my light on again and picked up my phone. This time, Lee answered.

"Elle?"

"Lee, I'm so sorry. I didn't want this to happen."

"Yeah, but it *has* happened, hasn't it?"

"I know. I made a terrible mistake. I thought it was better not to tell you. I was afraid of telling you, but I know it was wrong to lie to you." I was crying now. "Do you hate me?"

"I don't hate you . . . but I really don't like you much at the moment. Get some sleep now, Elle. See you in the morning."

"You mean . . . you're still giving me a ride to school?"

"Of course I am."

I started to cry even more then. "Goodnight," I said, when I could speak again. Then, "Lee? You know you're really important to me, don't you?"

"Yeah, I know. And I really care about you, too," he said. "But I don't have to like you all the time."

I was smiling now. "I know."

In the morning I raced downstairs as soon as I heard Lee's car. I jumped inside and threw my arms around his neck.

He laughed. "Nice to see you, too!" he said.

"Lee, please believe me. I really am sorry."

"I know," he said.

We sat in silence for a while. Then I said carefully, "Have you spoken to Noah since last night?"

"No. And I don't want to, either," he said. "He's made this mess. Now he can look after himself."

"Elle, Lee is the most important person in your life," I thought. "If you can't be with Noah and be friends with Lee, then you have to choose being friends with Lee."

At school, no one knew anything about what was happening. Everything was totally normal. But Noah wasn't there. On Tuesday I saw him at school, across the hall. I walked the other way. I knew from Lee that Noah was still not at home.

Then on Thursday I was coming out of the restrooms when I walked straight into Noah.

"Elle, we have to talk," he said. "Er . . . how are you?"

"Much better now that Lee has forgiven me."

"He hasn't forgiven me," Noah said. "I'm really sorry he found out like that. I hated seeing you so unhappy. I was lying to him, too. I made a mistake. I'm sorry. I haven't been able to sleep. I know you probably don't want to see me again . . ." He was speaking really quickly.

"Where have you been?" I asked him.

"In a hotel. I didn't want to make things worse for you with Lee. I've tried to forget about you. But I can't . . . I need you back. I can do it right this time."

He started to move closer to me and my heart jumped. What was he trying to tell me?

"Elle, Lee has just forgiven you. And now Noah wants to go on as before. That's crazy!"

Noah touched my hair.

"No, this is not happening. It can't."

"No," I said to Noah. His eyes were looking straight into mine.

"Elle, don't let him kiss you now because then you won't be able to be strong."

"No," I said again. "I have to go." And I ran away. Not because I was afraid of Noah. I was afraid of how I felt about him.

CHAPTER EIGHT
The summer dance

It was the day before the summer dance and I still didn't have a date.

"We can all go as friends, can't we?" Karen said. "We'll give you a ride, so you don't have to go alone."

The next evening I got ready for the dance. My dress was wonderful. I wasn't worried about not having a date and I felt great. I felt normal for the first time in weeks. But suddenly I thought about the other girls with their dates, and the photos that are always taken at dances. I felt a bit sad. I couldn't be in a photo without a date. Then I heard a knock at the front door. Karen and the others were early.

"Elle! They're here!" Dad called as he went to the door.

I stopped at the top of the stairs. I could hear Noah's voice.

"I need to speak to her," I heard him say.

"Well, she doesn't want to speak to you. You should leave," Dad replied. I heard the door close and I went downstairs.

"You look wonderful, Elle. When did my little girl grow up?" Dad said to me. Just then, there was another knock. I opened the door. Noah was standing there, wearing a black jacket with a white shirt and a narrow green tie which was the same colour as my dress. He looked amazing.

"What are you doing here?" I looked at him. His dark hair was falling into his eyes.

"I came to talk to you."

"Can you leave us alone for a minute?" I said to Dad.

Noah was down on one knee now, holding a white flower up to me.

"Elle Evans, will you be my date to the summer dance?"

I looked down at the flower and back to his face. How could I say no? "I don't know . . . I don't think it's a good idea," I said.

"Elle, forget what other people want for a minute. What do you want?"

So I took the flower. "Yes, Noah. I'll go to the dance with you," I told him.

I said goodbye to Dad and texted Karen. "I'm getting a ride. See you there."

We went out to Noah's car and he opened the door for me. Inside, he said, "I really care about you, Elle. I don't want to lose you again."

"This time, I must talk to Lee first," I said. "I can't lose my best friend."

We walked up to the hotel together, and no one knew who we were because of our masks. The dance room looked amazing. It had lovely white and silver decorations and around the sides of the room there were small round tables with beautiful white flowers. The dance floor was in the middle and there was a band on the stage.

In their masks, it was impossible to know who anyone was. The boys all looked the same in their black jackets.

Then I remembered Rachel's dress and found her in the crowd of people.

"I'm going to talk to Lee," I said to Noah.

But Rachel and Lee started dancing and I had to wait. Then Cody came over and asked me for a dance. After that, everyone took their seats for dinner. Each table had ten chairs around it. On my table, there were four girls and four boys, and me, with an empty chair next to me. Lee sat down on my other side. I had to find the right moment to tell him. My heart was going faster and faster.

"Elle! What's the matter?" Lee was saying. I jumped.

"Lee, can we talk? In private, I mean."

"OK, excuse us a minute, guys," Lee said to the others.

When we were outside the room, I said nervously, "Lee, promise me you won't get angry?"

"OK," he replied carefully.

"Noah came to my house earlier."

"What! What did he want?"

"To say sorry. Lee, I know you think it's crazy, but I want to be with him."

"He hurt you, Elle. He left you alone when I found out about you being together, when you were so unhappy."

"Lee, he tried to call, but I didn't answer."

"But is he right for you? I know what Noah's like."

"He makes me happy."

"Are you telling me you're in love with him?"

"No! Don't be ridiculous!" I laughed.

"I don't know, Elle," Lee said. There was a long silence before he spoke again. "But if it's what you want . . ."

"Really?" I put my arms around him. "Thanks, Lee. Thank you so much."

He smiled. "Let's go back. Dixon will steal my dinner if I'm not there." I laughed and followed him.

"Everything OK?" Dixon asked, when we got back to our table. Rachel looked at Lee and then smiled at me. I smiled back.

"Yeah," I said. "Everything's great."

After dinner, the dancing continued. I had no idea where Noah was. Then the music stopped and I heard a voice.

"Listen, please, everyone." Noah was on the stage, in the singer's place. What was he doing? Everybody was quiet, looking at him.

"I'm here to show someone I'm sorry," Noah said.

"Because I've done some stupid things. So . . . Elle? Where are you?"

Everyone looked at me. Even with my mask on, they knew where to find me.

"Elle, this is me saying sorry," Noah said. He turned to the band and they began to play a song called "I Really Want You," which was one of my favourites. Noah jumped off the stage and walked toward me.

"Elle Evans, will you be my girlfriend?" he said. Under my mask, my face went red, but I could not stop smiling. I could hear voices all around me.

"Sure. Why not?" I said. He laughed and pulled me into his arms.

"I just made myself look ridiculous for you, Elle," Noah whispered to me.

"Yeah, I know!" I laughed. "But you didn't have to."

"I wanted to. And I'm going to do things right this time." He moved closer and our lips met.

———

Later, I had a crowd of girls around me. "I'm so happy for you," Rachel said, smiling. Then I felt a strong arm pulling me onto the dance floor.

"Come on, Elle. The next song is the last one," Noah said, with his amazing smile. "We didn't have the first dance together, but nothing's going to stop me having the last dance with you."

CHAPTER NINE
We need to talk

School was finished for the summer. I was very happy being with Noah and I saw Lee a lot too – when he wasn't with Rachel.

One afternoon Lee and I were in my garden, planning our seventeenth birthdays.

"Let's have a costume party – we can go as Batman and Robin!" I said. I knew that Lee wanted a big party and I wanted to do something nice for him.

"Yes! It'll be so cool." Lee grinned.

Just then my phone rang. It was Noah.

"We need to talk," Noah said.

My heart stopped for a second. *"But that's what people say when they want to break up,"* I thought.

"Can you meet me at eight at Café Mario?"

"OK," I said. I was finding it hard to speak.

"What's wrong?" Lee asked, when I put my phone down.

"Noah said 'We need to talk.' Oh, Lee, we've just started dating, and now he's going to end it . . ."

"You don't know that. Maybe he just wants to talk?"

"But Lee, you know what those words mean. And . . . I think . . . I think I love him."

"I know," he said.

"How did you know before I did?" I asked, stupidly.

"Because I'm your other half," he answered. "Elle, it's

going to be OK because you have me. I'm here for you, always." He gave me a small, sad smile. "Now, do you want a ride to Café Mario?"

"Yes, please," I said, and I put my arms around him.

When we got to Café Mario, Noah's motorbike was already outside.

"Text me if you want me to come and get you," Lee said.

"Thanks, Lee." I could see Noah inside the café at a table by the window. He looked even more handsome than ever, in dark jeans and a white T-shirt. He actually stood up when I reached him.

I sat down and we both began to speak at the same time. We stopped and laughed nervously, and then a waiter came to take our order. At last, after our coffees arrived, Noah said, "We need to talk."

"Are you breaking up with me?" I asked, unable to hold the question in any longer.

"Listen, Elle. I've had a letter from Harvard – I have a place there."

"Harvard? *The* Harvard?"

He nodded.

"Wow. That's brilliant, Noah." I tried my best to sound happy.

"I know, but it's the other side of the country. And I don't have to go. I could go to college near here."

"Noah, you can't *not* go to Harvard! I'm happy for you. Really."

"But now there's this thing with you." He looked into

my eyes for a moment and he kissed me. Then he said, "I want to take you somewhere, and we need to go soon."

I laughed. "Where?"

"I'm not telling you. It's a surprise."

Then I remembered something. "No! I'm not going on the motorbike! Once was bad enough."

"Elle, you have to. I promise it will be OK. Please?" I looked into his blue eyes. How could I say no?

He put the helmet over my head and I put my arms around his waist, just like the first time. I kept my eyes shut.

"*I hate this. I hate this. I hate this.*

I love him. I love him. I love him."

When we stopped, everything went silent. We were in a park at the bottom of a hill, outside the city. We climbed off the motorbike and Noah started walking up the hill.

"Where are we going?"

"You'll see," he answered.

It didn't take us long to reach the top. We sat down under a big tree and I realized why we were here. This place looked over half the city and you could see the beaches and the ocean, too. It looked beautiful, and now that the sun was going down, the sky was turning red. The clouds were pink and silver. There was no noise, just the sound of the leaves moving above our heads.

"Wow," I said. "It's amazing."

"Like you," Noah said. He looked into my eyes for the longest moment. "I love you, Elle."

I couldn't say anything. I put my head against his.

"I love you," I whispered back, at last.

"*He loves me,*" I thought. "*I'm in love with my best friend's brother . . . and he loves me back.*"

"Elle?" I woke up from my dream. "What are we going

to do? About me going to Harvard?" Noah asked.

"You really want to go, don't you?"

After a while he said, "Yes, I want to go. But I don't want to leave you."

"I don't want you to leave me either," I said. "But you have to go. We both know it."

He kissed the side of my head and said, "I love you."

On our seventeenth birthdays Lee and I had lunch together with our families, like we always did on our birthdays. After lunch we opened our presents. Everyone laughed when Lee gave me the same T-shirt as the one I gave him, but in a different colour. And our costume party in the evening was amazing.

But the party ended too quickly and the days of summer flew by. I tried not to think about Noah leaving. I didn't want to put a dark cloud over our last few weeks together.

And then we were at the airport, saying goodbye.

"I guess this is it," Lee said, putting his hand on Noah's shoulder. "Good luck."

"Be good and work hard, son," said Noah's dad.

"Call us when you get there," said his mom. She was trying not to cry, and she wasn't the only one. I didn't want Noah to go. But it wasn't my choice to make – I knew he had to go.

I walked ahead with Noah to say goodbye to him alone.

"It'll be all right. I'll see you in a few weeks," he said. "But it's not going to be easy without you."

I put my arms around him and held him close. I wanted to remember that feeling of his arms around me, his face in my hair.

"I love you," he whispered in my ear.

"I love you," I said, trying hard not to cry. "So much."

We kissed and it felt like my heart might break. Then we stayed there, our heads still touching.

"I have to go," he whispered.

"Good luck, Noah."

He grinned at me. "Hey, Rochelle, you forget. You're talking to Flynn – I don't need luck!"

I laughed. He walked away and disappeared into the crowd of other travellers.

"I'll be OK," I thought. *"Lee will be by my side. I want to be in love with Noah forever. But I can't see into the future, so right now I'm just happy to be in love with Noah."*

A little later, I stood by the windows, watching the plane. I felt someone at my side, putting an arm around me. It was Lee.

"Just think," he said. "All this started with a kissing booth." And we laughed.

Penguin Readers

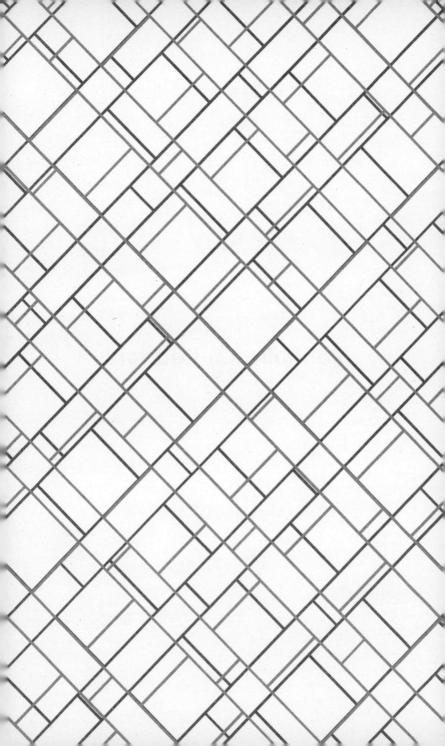

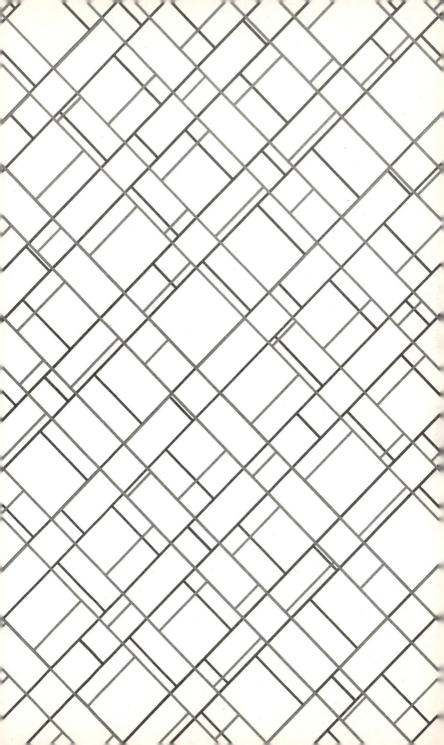